I0586650

SUCKERS

Prequel

Releasing A Vampire

Jacky Dahlhaus

Folla Fiction Publishing

First published online: August 2017
First published in print: September 2018

eBook ISBN: 978-0-9956719-8-0
Print ISBN: 978-0-9956719-2-8

Book cover design by David Williams, edited by Jacky Dahlhaus

jackydahlhaus.com

This book is a work of fiction. All characters and events in this publication, other than those clearly in the public domain, are fictitious and any resemblance to real persons, living or dead, is purely coincidental.

Books written by Jacky Dahlhaus:

Releasing A Vampire

Living Like A Vampire

Raising A Vampire

Killing A Vampire

Short Shockers

jackydahlhaus.com

Contents

Friday Afternoon, May 7th, 2004
Fort Sam Houston, San Antonio, Texas

Colonel Terrence J. Henderson, T.J. to his close friends, strode into the conference room with confidence. It was his second year in charge of the U.S. Army Medical Research Institute of Infectious Diseases (USAMRIID) and he ran the place as smooth as full-fat vanilla ice cream. That's what was on his mind, ice cream. As soon as he would be home he'd make himself one, in a fancy dessert glass. He would put three scoops of vanilla ice cream into the glass, pour chocolate sauce over them, and put in a chocolate flake. He'd possibly pour some brandy over the whole and sprinkle some crushed hazelnut over it too. Maybe not. He'd have to see how he felt about the hazelnut at the time. It also depended if he had some left over in the pantry. He couldn't remember.

Henderson liked eating ice cream. Not that he had a lot of time to do so. Work kept him in the office most hours and inside the building it seemed like they were trying to recreate the North Pole, not exactly the place to eat ice cream.

As soon as Henderson sat down, the room became

quiet. He checked the faces of the attendees and saw the usual staff sitting around the large conference table. It was going to be an ordinary Friday afternoon meeting, with the ordinary last-minute requests. They always wanted so much from him. Most of all decisions they didn't want to make themselves. That heavy burden always fell on him. 'Just as well they pay me accordingly, so I can eat expensive ice creams while sitting in my Jacuzzi at home,' he thought.

"What's the first point on the agenda?" Henderson asked his secretary.

James Brown, not the one you immediately think of but another, much less famous one, put a piece of paper in front of his boss.

"Nine items today," James said. "Most of them to do with the new building equipment and one new project request." He put his hands on his laptop, ready to take notes.

Henderson's eyes drifted down to item number five on the agenda. 'Request to start Project Duchenne,' it read. He sat up straighter. His cousin twice removed, a boy named Boyd, had muscular dystrophy. Henderson was immediately interested in what Project Duchenne was and couldn't wait to hear more about it.

Unfortunately, the meeting went on and on, with lots of arguing about money. Most of the time the meetings were about money. Had money not been an issue, it would have been a lot faster to get things done and the army would have functioned very differently. As it was, the spending of every cent had to be fought for.

When the meeting finally arrived at item number five, Henderson sat upright again from his position that had become slumped over the last two hours.

"Who is in charge of Project Duchenne?" Henderson asked.

A woman at the back of the room put her hand up. Henderson hadn't seen her earlier. How could he have missed her? He took in her mousy brown hair, pulled back into a ponytail, her face devoid of makeup, and her camouflage uniform that almost disappeared in the mass of uniforms in the room, as it was designed to do. 'That's why,' he thought as he forced himself to be interested in this woman, who appeared to have gone through great trouble not to look like a woman.

Henderson liked women to look like women. He didn't like it at all when they tried to look like men. He was convinced that women were smarter than men and that was why, through the ages, men had tried their hardest to make sure women didn't realize this. Making them dress up in the most uncomfortable shoes and pieces of clothing and have them put paint on their faces was part of that plan. It had worked so far. Women who didn't comply with this visual standard had too much time on their hand for thinking about other things. Like why they weren't treated the same or paid as much as men. These women were dangerous to the status quo.

"Who are you?" Henderson asked the plain looking woman.

"Stephanie Bonnetti, virologist and biological weapons expert," she replied. Without blinking, she stared back at Colonel Henderson. She knew that look on his face all too well. She had come a long way since joining the army and had seen it in many men's eyes. It had a hint of detest and a lot of aggression. It hadn't deterred her from becoming the best she could be, which happened to be better than most men. She had been lucky to have been born with an excellent memory and very logic thinking. In time, the men she had met had all realized her worth and hadn't stood in her way to serve her country to her best ability. She would make an extra effort to add Colonel Henderson to her string of admirers.

"We are hoping," Dr. Bonnetti began to explain, "to create a virus that will enhance the cellular production of a protein called dystrophin, which will result in increased muscle mass. This could be extremely beneficial to muscle dystrophy sufferers, but also create more muscle mass in healthy persons, like soldiers of the Special Forces. If we can make it work, we could also offer it to Navy Seals, the Marine Special Operations Command Officers, and the Air Force Tactics Forces as well."

The heads in the room turned from Dr. Bonnetti to Colonel Henderson as if they were at a tennis match. Colonel Henderson in return turned his head and stared out of the window, letting everyone wait for his response. He didn't care about that. He also didn't care about the soldiers of the other forces. All he cared about were the ground troops. So often they were overlooked. Navy SEALs this, Air Force Officers that. What about the ground troops? They were doing most of the work, keeping things going in this country, doing most of the work to keep people safe. It was time to let them shine for a change. Apart from doing something that could possibly help his cousin Boyd. He faced Dr. Bonnetti again.

"How likely is it that this is going to work?" Henderson asked.

Dr. Bonnetti shuffled some paperwork she had brought and pulled a piece of paper to the front.

She studied it for a moment and when she looked up, she said, "The possibility of success is seventy-nine percent."

"Do it," was Henderson's reply.

The remainder of the meeting was about where to get the money from to do it.

Friday Afternoon, August 6th, 2004
Portland

The sun shone brightly, and I was about to move from my parental home in Portland, Maine, to Bullsbrook, a small countryside town not too far away. I was twenty-two and had finished my teaching degree in June. I had secured a position as a science teacher at Bullsbrook High and was looking forward to starting my new life in the idyllic town. I counted myself lucky as not a lot of positions were available in towns like Bullsbrook. To get one first go was like winning the lottery. Everybody from my class envied me. Some fellow-students had even offered to trade places with me, but I had refused their bribes. Of course, I had invited them all to come and visit me once I had settled in. I was already looking forward to catching up with my university friends and exchanging teaching experiences. Moving out on my own scared me a little and the thought of having my friends over soon kept me going.

Mom and Dad had dreaded the day of our parting. Even though they had always jokingly asked my two sisters and me when we were finally going to leave so they could have their own life back, they were sad to see me go for real. I was the last one to leave, and it wasn't a happy occasion anymore. My oldest sister, Maxine, had left years ago. She had married a naval officer and moved from naval base to naval base with him. We didn't keep in contact much due to the age difference. Six years is a big age gap. Julie, who was two only years younger than me, hadn't studied and didn't get hitched but still wanted to leave home as soon as possible after she had finished high school. Mom had been adamant and very persuasive in keeping her at home for another few years, but Julie's spirit couldn't be tamed, and she had left last year when she received a position in an office in the countryside. I never knew exactly what she was doing in what sort of office. Every time I asked her, my thoughts drifted off as soon as she started the narrative of her answer. Her habit of jam-packing her stories with little details nobody was ever interested in made your mind seek refuge elsewhere. If somebody would have mentioned the name of the office, I was sure I'd recognize it though. Whatever she was doing, she seemed happy, and that was all that was important to me. We didn't keep in touch as often as I wanted to either, but I heard most of her stories through my parents. They were always keeping me up to date with news from my sisters.

Mom and Dad stood on their porch to wave me off. As I walked to my car, I was amazed at the amount of stuff that filled it. I had thought I didn't own much yet my humble belongings took up about all the space safe the driver's seat. Mom had promised me a few days earlier they would come and visit me as soon as possible. She'd said she didn't want to interfere with me finding myself in this new town, so they had planned to be over in about a fortnight. The thought of them visiting so soon had made me anxious. I had lain awake at night, tossing and turning with the thought of them coming over when my house would be a mess and my teaching preparations taking up all of my free time. With dread, I had tried my luck and asked to stretch it to four weeks. I had nearly fallen off my chair when she agreed.

Mom is the best Mom in the world, but sometimes she can be a little overprotective of her nestlings, so I thought she was very brave to let me, the last one, leave the parental house. I knew it would be so empty without any of us three living at home. The thought had crossed my mind to ask for a teaching job in the city and live at home to keep Mom and Dad company, but when this position in Bullsbrook came up, it was an offer I couldn't refuse. Mom had cried when I had read out the acceptance letter and Dad had hugged her, kissing her hair and telling her everything would be alright. I had felt like the 'Daughter of Doom,' but when Dad had looked at me, his eyes had told me that he and Mom would be okay. Dad never talked a lot, but I knew he loved Mom very much and I was sure that together they could withstand all storms, so to speak.

I stuffed the last item, my childhood teddy bear, in the car before walking back to say my final goodbye.

Dad had his arm around Mom's waist as they stood on their porch.

"Please drive carefully, darling," Mom said.

"Nope, I'm going to hit every lamp post on the way, I think," I joked as I stepped onto the porch.

"Oh, you know what I mean, silly," and she put her arms around me in a big hug. "Make sure to give us a call when you arrive. I'll be worried sick if I don't know you've arrived safely."

"I will, Mom, I will," I soothed her as I kissed her goodbye. When she let go of me, I gave Dad a hug and a kiss.

"Don't do anything I wouldn't do, kid," Dad said with a smile on his face. He never called me Kate, I was always his 'kid.'

"Well, that basically means I can do anything I want." I couldn't help the huge grin on my face.

Mom poked Dad in the ribs with her elbow and gave him her angry stare.

"Ouch!" Dad pretended to be hurt. He quickly replaced his arm around Mom's waist though. "Are you sure you don't want us to come and help?" Dad asked.

"No, I'm sure. I'll be alright," I replied. Again. It wasn't the first time he'd asked.

I went back to my car and they both waved as I reversed off their driveway. I honked my horn and waved one more time out of the window before I drove off. I missed them already.

Friday Evening, August 6th, 2004
Bullsbrook

By the time I arrived in Bullsbrook, it was early evening. The trip had only been a few hours' drive from Portland, but it had been halfway into the afternoon when I left my parent's place. Mom had done everything in her power to keep me there for as long as she could. This included preparing a cooked lunch which resulted in me leaving later than I had planned.

I had no trouble getting to my new hometown with the help of the map on my cell phone. Once I arrived in Bullsbrook, I had to pull over to find the exact location of my new abode. It turned out I wasn't far from it and after turning three more corners, I saw it. It was the spitting image of a house from a fairy tale. It had a black, shingled roof, white trimmings, red weatherboard walls, and an immaculate green lawn lay in front of it. It was love at first sight. It was tiny, but I knew I was going to be happy here.

The owner and landlady, Mrs. Babcock, had told me she lived next door and that I could pick up the keys from her place when I arrived. I parked the car in my driveway and crossed the manicured lawn to Mrs. Babcock's front door. As I stepped onto her porch, I mused about her name.

Such a weird name, but it could have been a lot worse if the second 'b' had been a 'd.'

I knocked on the front door, stepped back, and waited. The thought entered my mind that I should have let her know what time I would be arriving. Panic squeezed my chest as I thought of the possibility she may not be at home right now. Bingo was a favorite past-time of the elderly. At least, that's what Mum once said, much to the annoyance of Dad who had said he'd rather die an early age than play bingo. I peered through the front window to try and detect any sign of life.

To my relief, the front door opened, and I felt a bit embarrassed spying into her home. I stepped back to the door and smiled. In the doorway stood a little, old lady who also looked as if she stepped right out of a fairytale. She didn't look like a wicked witch, more like a fairy godmother. She had a tiny, fragile frame and wore a bright turquoise dress with a white, lace collar. Her white hair was stuck up in a huge bun on the back of her head.

Would she topple forward if her hair was cut off?

As I worked on my first impression of my landlady, the old woman did the same of her new tenant. Her eyes, that had a sweet sparkle in them, went up and down as they took me in. When they finally settled on my face, looking at me through gold-rimmed reading glasses which were balanced halfway on her delicate nose, she smiled at me.

"You must be the new teacher," she said. Her voice was sweet and melodious with a distinct English accent.

"Yes, I'm Kate Clarke. It's so nice to meet you, Mrs. Babcock," I replied and stuck my hand out.

She took my hand and shook it. Her grip felt remarkably strong for such a tiny frame.

"The pleasure's all mine," she said. "Come on in, dearie. Would you like a cup of tea?"

Although I liked the little, old lady, I had to refuse her offer. There was so much I still needed and wanted to do before I could go to sleep.

"I'm so sorry," I said, "but I have a lot to unpack. Some other time perhaps?" I bit my lip in anticipation of her reaction.

"Not to worry, love. You must be eager to settle in. They always are. Let me find the keys for you," and she indicated I follow her into her home. It was very light inside. The decor seemed from the nineteen-forties, but everything was painted white. Mrs. Babcock opened a cupboard in her living room and rummaged around in it.

"Thank you so much for renting out the house to me. I am so grateful. It looks lovely."

"Thank you, dearie. I always only rent it out to teachers, you know. I've never had any regrets." She opened another cupboard. "Now where did I put them..." she murmured. "All teachers have always been very well-behaved people and have taken really good care of the property." She opened a drawer from the sideboard now.

I felt my cheeks become flushed. "I hope I won't let you down. I've never lived on my own, you know." Automatically, my thumb went to my mouth to bite the skin next to the nail. When I became aware of performing my nasty habit, I swung my arm down. I clasped my hands behind my back, just in case.

"I'm sure you'll manage," Mrs. Babcock smiled as she turned to me with keys in her hand. As I stuck out my hand, she took it and put the keys in it. Before she let go, she said, "But you know where I live, and you can always come over if you need help with anything. Or if you just fancy a cup of tea of course." She giggled.

Her whole demeanor was so sweet. I couldn't help but laugh with her. "Thank you, I will."

She let me out and I walked back to my car. She waved to me, and I waved to her in return, before she went back inside. I made myself a promise to have a cup of tea with Mrs. Babcock at least once a week.

I grabbed the box with groceries from the passenger seat of my car and walked toward my new home. When I stepped onto the porch out the front, I made a turn on my axis while inspecting the place. The area seemed big enough to put a chair and table here to enjoy the setting sun. Happy about my second impression, I had a small setback when I struggled to turn the key in the lock of the front door and hold the box upright at the same time. I didn't let this little thing bring me down and when I managed to turn the key, I finally stepped inside.

It's a pity I can't carry myself over the threshold.

My grin went even wider than it already was. My new home was small but cozy. I stood in an L-shaped living room and, like in Mrs. Babcock's home, I felt as if I had stepped into a time machine, taking me to the fifties this time. I rented the house with furniture because I didn't own any myself yet. There was a red, faux-leather couch and chairs, all with wooden legs and metal end bits. A metal-rimmed, bean-shaped coffee table with a strange, colored pattern on a black background on its surface, matching side tables, and wooden cabinets of a matching style. All were in a good state and gave the room a homely feel. Apart from the pink paint on the walls. I would have to do something about that. I popped the grocery box down on the coffee table. A separate room occupied the right-hand quadrant and I opened the door for a peek. It appeared to be my bedroom. I liked the white, metal double bed. It made the whole room have a romantic feel. The nightstand next to it, the dresser, and a wardrobe were also white. Definitely a touch from Mrs. Babcock. I opened the doors of the cabinets, one after the other. They would give me ample of space to put my stuff in.

I returned to the living room and found the small kitchen at the back of it. It was more a kitchenette size-wise, to be honest, but it had a full stove and sink. The granite countertop had seen better days, with chips off here and there, but it was clean and functional. Through a side door in the kitchen, I found the bathroom. It also was small yet contained a shower/bath combination. I could already picture myself having a relaxing bubble bath every week. The bathroom wasn't ensuite, but as I didn't have to share my home with anybody else, I didn't care. I picked up the grocery box from the living room and began unloading my groceries into the refrigerator and kitchen cupboards. Mrs. Babcock had been so kind to switch on the refrigerator earlier. I couldn't help but smile when I realized I was putting *my* groceries into *my* refrigerator in *my* kitchen in *my* new home.

Such happiness with such a mundane action.

Even if it is a rental.

I went back to my car and made several trips to move all of my stuff from the car into the house. When I had unpacked the essentials and stored them in the appropriate places, I was knackered. I went into the bedroom, kicked off my shoes, and let myself fall onto my back on the bed. It squeaked, even under my tiny frame. By now it was dark in the room but for a tiny sliver of light coming from above. I tilted my head up and noticed one little, high window on the outer wall, mostly covered by a white blackout blind. I wondered why. The window was too high for anybody to peek inside. I gathered a previous renter must have liked to sleep in.

I relaxed again and felt happy. I spread my arms and legs out to all four corners of the mattress and began moving them as if making a snow angel. I laughed. To have this place all to myself was like being a queen in a palace. My palace!

Saturday, August 7th, 2004
Biosafety Level 2 Laboratory, unknown location

Dr. Bonnetti crossed the medical facility's parking lot with a spring in her step. She couldn't wait to get to the lab. They had injected the rats with the genetically engineered Adeno-Associated Virus the day before and she was eager to know how they were doing. The virus was not harmful in itself, but you just never knew. Hopefully, none of the rats had become ill. Any eye or nasal discharge or rattling lung noises would mean the virus hadn't worked. The virus was supposed to create more muscle protein once it injected its genetically modified DNA into muscle cells, not replicate any unhealthy habits. Bonnetti wasn't a religious person, but her Catholic upbringing got the better of her and she prayed under her breath as she entered the building.

Once she had donned her lab coat, gloves, and face shield, she entered the room where the rats were kept. Jen Lam, the lab technician, was already checking the animals.

"How are my lovely pumpkin horses performing today?" Dr. Bonnetti asked Jennifer.

Jen looked up at her boss. 'Why is she talking to me while I'm trying to listen to the rat's breathing,' she thought. 'She should know better.' Jen finished her lung exam, took the stethoscope out of her ears, and draped the instrument around her neck. "They seem to be doing fine," she said. She smiled at Dr. Bonnetti, who thought that Jen's words were music to her ears and was nearly dancing around the room.

Jen was as happy with the result as Dr. Bonnetti was, but not for the same reasons. Jennifer had become a laboratory animal technician because she loved animals. It would take her a week of grieving when the rats had to be put down. Whether the treatments were working or not, none of them ever survived the projects. She had had to put down an awful lot of rats in the past, but she had always done it with love and care, or speed, which basically came down to the same thing. Jen always thought of the bigger picture, of all the people the rats would be saving by giving their lives to science. It was the only way to stay on top of it, the only way not to succumb to the repetitive grief.

Together, the two women kept an eye on the rats for the rest of the day and the following weeks. Body temperatures were measured, as well as weights and leg circumferences. An eye was kept out for conjunctivitis, rhinitis, and any signs of lung involvement. All seemed to go as planned. None of the rats became sick although they did lose some due to aggression. Jen had never experienced this amount of fighting amongst the animals. It was known that too many rats in too small a cage would instigate aggression, but they had kept to the regulations of only two per cage. Some didn't fight at all, but if they did, it was always to the death. She thought it very strange. Dr. Bonnetti dismissed Jen's concerns and said it to be within normal parameters.

Once the trial was over, all the rats were euthanized and dissected. Muscle tissue was taken from every rat and studied under the microscope. The results were unanimous; the virus treatment was a success.

Saturday, August 7th, 2004
Bullsbrook

Before I had left home, Mom had advised me to paint my interior before unpacking too many boxes. I had discussed it early Saturday morning with Mrs. Babcock and she had agreed for me to paint the living room walls as long as I did it to a good standard. So I went out to find the local paint shop. I learned my first lesson of country living as there wasn't a paint shop in town. Instead, they had the Happy Hardware store, where you could find most DIY material, including paint.

There, I saw Sue for the first time. We met when we bumped into each other trying to pick up the same can of corn-yellow paint from a top shelf.

"Oh, sorry, you go ahead and take it. I'll take the one behind it," was the first thing she said to me.

Her voice had an uplifting ring to it and hearing it made me even happier than I already was. I looked sideways to find out who this beautiful voice belonged to and my mouth fell open. She was the most colorful girl I had ever seen. She wore a yellow painters' overall, purple army boots with red shoelaces, and a rainbow-colored, long-sleeved shirt.

"No way, you go ahead and take this one. I'll take the one behind it," I said apologetically and stepped back to give her more space.

"Okay, thanks," she said and lifted the can off by the handle with ease. She didn't even have to stand on her tippy toes to do so. She stepped back to let me grab the next can. To my embarrassment, I was too short and couldn't reach it, not even on my tippy toes. I looked over my shoulder to see if she was still there and noticed she was indeed. She smiled a big smile at me.

Please go away and let me embarrass myself without an audience.

"Don't worry, I can do this," I said as I re-adjusted my handbag and did my best ballet impression. Holding myself up with one hand on the shelf post, I let my other hand make grabbing movements in the space where the first can had been, trying to locate the second one. Instead of a prima ballerina, I felt like an orangutan hanging off a tree. When I peeked over my shoulder again to see if I still had an audience watching my animal escapade, my eyes met hers. There was a brightness in hers, a happiness that spread to her cheekbones and her broad smile. I realized how stupid I must have looked and we both began laughing out loud, her long dreadlocks bouncing up and down. Less embarrassed now, but only slightly, I stepped back again, and she pushed the paint can she was holding into my hands and easily grabbed the next one from the shelf. She secured the can on her hip and turned to me.

"I'm Sue. I'm the new English teacher at the local

high school," she said.

"No way, I'm Kate, the new science teacher," I replied to my soon-to-be-colleague.

"Wow, I can't believe you're also new here. I thought I was going to be able to blend in quietly on my own."

I didn't blink for a few seconds, the sudden silence awkward. Then, Sue threw her head back and laughed a beautiful, full laugh.

"No need to keep it in, peeshwanck. I can take it," she said as she wiped tears away from the corners of her eyes.

"Yeah, sorry. I didn't want to offend you, but you're not exactly camouflaged," and I indicated her whole being as I smiled.

"I know," she said as she inspected herself. "Life's too short to be restricted by conventionality. You should try letting go. It's liberating. Say, where's your koté, your home?"

I told her the location of my new home and we began chatting. It appeared Sue rented an apartment not far from mine and was also re-decorating. She invited me over to her place for a cuppa which I gladly accepted. I was so happy to have found a friend. Sue was completely into purples and pinks but wanted the yellow paint for her kitchen cabinet doors. I stayed the rest of the day to help her paint them.

We got on really well and we helped each other

paint our new homes and gave each other tips on decorating. Of course, Sue would have turned my house into a multicolored circus attraction if I had taken all of her advice, but fortunately, she was not offended when I settled for more muted fall colors such as corn-yellow and orange. These went well with my red furniture.

From that first day on, we had dinner together most of the time until school started. Her cuisine was very different from what I cooked for her. Hers included lots of things that I had never heard of, like gumbo's, boudin, and tasso. My mother's cooking had been extremely bland—to keep Dad happy—and Sue's dishes were a revelation for the senses. I didn't appreciate *all* the food she put in front of me. She once fed me something so spicy, the tears were rolling over both our cheeks. Over mine, because I felt like my insides were on fire, and over hers, because she had one look at my face and couldn't stop laughing. Once I extinguished the flames with some cold yogurt drink she had quickly made for me, I had one look at her and we both burst out laughing again. Whenever one of us mentioned fish from that moment on, we would both laugh.

August was wonderful with plenty of hot days and balmy nights. We often sat on our porches after dinner, enjoying a glass of wine and exchanging teaching tactics and experiences from our training days. We regularly discussed the plumber Sue had had to call in to fix a leaking sink. Apparently, he was a looker and she described me every detail of his cute butt that she studied intently when he had his head stuck in the kitchen cupboard.

Life was good.

Monday, August 30th, 2004
Bullsbrook

My first day as a teacher began on Monday, the 30th of August. Bullsbrook High was large for a country school as it also housed the adult education center for the area. The double story, main building loomed in front of me as I walked up to it from the staff parking lot. I had felt extremely anxious on Sunday, but there had been no need for it as the first day at school was a 'teachers-only' day. I had a reprieve from the students' judgment for another day.

We sat through the morning meeting in the staff room. Our Head Master, Mr. Finkle, went through the year's aims and budgets. He also introduced the new teachers to the existing staff; Sue, myself, and a guy named Charlie. Charlie was the new Industrial Arts teacher. Most teachers greeted us with a friendly smile, but I noticed some didn't smile at Charlie. I sure hoped it had nothing to do with him being a dwarf.

After a private tour of the buildings by one of the teachers, Sue, Charlie, and I sat together in the staff room for lunch. My guess was that Charlie was about ten years older than Sue and me. I asked him how he became an Arts teacher and he told us he used to be a silversmith. After years of struggling to sell his creations on markets and fairs, he had realized he could hardly earn enough money to sustain a normal living, let alone a pension. Hence he had re-schooled to become an Arts teacher.

"What kind of jewelry did you make?" Sue asked.

"Rings mostly," Charlie answered, "but also necklaces, earrings, and belly button piercings. You need any?" Charlie smiled.

I looked at Sue, who shook her head.

"Sorry, me neither," I said to Charlie. I pointed at the rings on his hands. "Did you make those yourself?"

"Sure did. They all have their own story, but I won't bother you with those." He smiled a mysterious smile.

"I like the dragon one," Sue said.

"I like the Celtic one," I blurted out after Sue's comment. I didn't mean to overshadow her remark and I hoped I didn't hurt her feelings.

Charlie glanced at me for a moment and seemed to understand my expression as he first mentioned to Sue how much time and tries it had taken him to make the dragon ring. It was made with a mold. Then he told us he made the Celtic ring to remind him of his Irish background.

"How do you get the metal strings woven and connected without a seam visible?" I asked him.

Charlie explained that they actually weren't woven. "You make the ring from a rectangular sheet of metal which you weld into a closed band. The trick is to make it so the seam doesn't show." He took the ring off his finger and showed us that there was indeed no seam to be seen, inside or out. "Then you punch holes in calculated locations and file the remaining silver strands to look like they're woven over and under each other."

"Wow! That must take forever," Sue said amazed.

Charlie laughed. "Yes, it kind of does, but it's so worth it!" He beamed as he admired his own ring.

The ring truly looked marvelous.

I liked Charlie. Like Sue, he was easy to talk to and I felt at ease whenever he was nearby. Even though he was almost ten years older than Sue and me, he was one of us. He liked our kind of music and made the same type of jokes. We were a great team, the three of us, having lunches and dinners together, exchanging teaching experiences, and relaxing on Friday nights at the local bar. We called ourselves the three musketeers and toasted to ourselves at every round.

September 20th, 2004, Monday
Biosafety Level 2 Laboratory, unknown location

The man wearing a green beret saluted Dr. Bonnetti.

"Officer D.I.M. Becker, 3rd Infantry Division, 1st Armored Brigade Combat Team, 3rd Combined Arms Battalion, 69th Armor Regiment, at your service." He yelled his name and rank more than say it. Such was standard amongst green berets and other special operations forces. It basically said these were men not to play with.

The fact that the initials of his first names, David Ian Michael, spelled 'dim' hadn't helped his initial time with the armed forces. Everybody had assumed he also *was* dim and had treated him as such. The fact that he had an IQ of 140 had helped David to overcome this hardship and he soon had earned respect from his fellow trainees. By the end of the Q Course, he had earned the nickname 'Gov,' and even though each and every Green Beret was trained to make instant decisions in a variety of circumstances, all of David's troop officers looked at him for advice whenever a decision had to be made and they gladly accepted that he was made their Commander.

David had cried when his troop of Green Berets had told him they would join him as a volunteer for this new virus test. They knew his little boy had a brain tumor and needed expensive treatment. The extra money David would make by participating wouldn't be enough and he hadn't wanted to let his mates down by leaving them, but what choice did he have? When his troop told him that they would join his cause and donate their extra income toward his son's operation, the closeness between the men felt like a bunch of sardines in a tin. You really couldn't get much closer than that.

"Yeah, yeah," Dr. Bonnetti said. "Just get undressed. Leave your clothes on the chair and step on the scales."

Becker did as he was told. He didn't bat an eye when he stood naked in front of the woman. He was trained to obey orders. Besides, he didn't mind showing off his perfect body at all. He loved how his muscles gleamed with sweat after a workout in the gym. He admired how well-proportioned he was and how strong and athletic he looked. His manhood was also something to be proud of. His wife had often told him so, before, during, and after their lovemaking.

It appeared that Becker was an excellent specimen to do the virus test on. He passed all the intake parameters as did most of his comrades. Only Milton was rejected because of a high level of protein they found in his urine. They sent him home to have further testing done to find the cause of it. Becker fist-bumped the others when he came out, dressed in a hospital-staff-type uniform, at the end of the corridor. The end where only the test bunnies were allowed to go.

"Speed and Power!" Becker said to his troop.

"Speed and Power!" was the synced reply.

During the next few days, the green berets were more minutely measured, and their strength and stamina tested to their limits. Their test results were far higher than the average gym-goer could dream of and it was almost impossible to think they could be improved at all. Overall spirits were high. They were told what the test was supposed to do, and they were looking forward to it. They would become the elite of the elite. What was there not to like?

Thursday, September 23rd, 2004
Bullsbrook

Sometimes Charlie was in a dark mood. Sue was more like a bouncy Spaniel, always happy and ready for some fun. If Charlie had been a dog, I guess he would have been more like an English Bulldog; very happy and bouncy at times, but with a calm, quiet side too. Almost sulky.

"What's up with you?" I asked him one day when he didn't laugh at one of Sue's jokes.

"Forget it," he said and turned away.

I couldn't forget it though, so when we walked out of the school building that day, I invited him over for dinner.

Charlie arrived that evening carrying a bottle. He handed me the Californian wine 'as a token of gratitude for the invitation.' I thought he sounded a bit formal and decided to ignore the remark. Together we made my self-invented ratatouille-spaghetti dish. As Charlie was a vegetarian, I left out the bacon that I normally would have added. It didn't taste the same without it, but Charlie thought it was scrumptious nevertheless. He was his funny self again and we had lots of fun in a competition of who could slurp up a spaghetti strand the fastest. After dinner, with a large glass of the sweet

31

wine he brought, we were sitting inside, enjoying the comfort of my warm home as fall made it too cold to sit on the porch. Fortunately, we could still enjoy the setting sun through the window. A silence fell after we closed the topic of how to integrate less bright students into the curriculum.

"So, why do you walk around with a rain cloud over your head now and again?" I asked as I swirled the wine in my glass.

I felt his gaze on me. I didn't see what his face looked like and so had no idea what he thought about me raising the subject. Charlie remained silent.

Only one way to find out, Kate.

I took another sip of wine before I looked at him. I kept my face as blank as possible. We made eye contact but as quick as he did, Charlie turned his head and stared into the sunset. I didn't move, and Charlie still didn't say anything. His gaze finally dropped down to his wine glass.

"I'd rather not talk about it," he finally said with much less enthusiasm than he had previously shown when talking about our teaching topic.

Oh dear, this is more serious than I thought.

I took a deep breath. I wasn't going to take no for an answer. I knew something bothered him and I wasn't going to let him suffer in silence. I let my breath out slowly.

"That's okay, Charlie, but you know a shared pain is

32

half the pain. You know I am here for you if you need me." I didn't want to push him too much as I knew that wouldn't work for sure.

Another silence followed.

I was about to get up to get the bottle from the refrigerator for a refill when Charlie decided to share his pain.

"It's some of the teachers at school. They are giving me a hard time." He sighed.

I stared at him without blinking. When my eyes felt like they were going to shrivel up, I blinked a few times.

"What do you mean? Why?" A deep frown now on my face.

I was surprised about what he had just said. All the other teachers were so nice to me.

"Oh, it started quite innocent. At the beginning of the year, a few of them made remarks behind my back about my short arms and legs."

Charlie had been born with achondroplasia, the most common form of dwarfism. This meant his body couldn't make bone out of cartilage which affected the long bones the most. As a result, he had short arms, and short, curved legs, amongst other problems.

"Silly things like 'I wonder which one of Snow White's dwarves he is, or 'where does he keep his pony that gives him his bowlegs.'"

He looked at me now, expecting a reaction, but for a change, I was lost for words. My mouth had dropped

33

open and all I managed to say after a while was, "That's so wrong."

"Tell me about it, but that's humans for you. Welcome to the real world. I've heard stuff like that all my life and have learned to live with it, you know," he continued. "People stare at me everywhere I go." He took another sip from his wine.

I still couldn't believe that my colleagues could be so cruel. I would have expected it from the students. I knew kids could be vicious in their remarks. I didn't expect it from the people who were supposed to teach the children to accept each individual for their merits, not for their looks.

"Since last week it has progressed into bumping into me on purpose and making the excuse that they didn't see me."

"Nooo! You've got to be kidding me."

"It's true," Charlie replied, and he showed me a couple of bumps on his head. They were big bumps. They made me so angry. How can these people be so mean?

"You've got to tell Mr. Finkle about this."

"Been there, done that," Charlie said with a heavy sigh, "but Mr. Finkle chose not to believe my story. He can't believe that his best and oldest teachers would do something like this." He took another sip from his glass.

I was stumped. "What about the Board of Teachers,

surely they'd make work of it?" I tried.

He shook his head and said, "Forget it, Kate. I don't want to make an issue out of it. It'll pass."

I wasn't so sure about it. As I frowned into the sunset, I couldn't stop worrying. I wanted Charlie to be happy here, just like I was. I crossed my arms and breathed out through my nostrils.

"Look, what would be the outcome?" Charlie said as he repositioned himself on the couch, leaning forward. "That they transfer me to another school? That they reprimand the teachers which will make them hate me even more? I like living here and don't want to move. I have traveled enough in my lifetime and I want to settle down." From the corner of my eye, I saw he opened his mouth to say something else, but he must have decided against it. I turned my head to him to encourage him to say what he wanted to say. Instead, Charlie sat back and without making eye contact he said, "I will just have to deal with it," and he made a movement with both his hands as if to say, 'and that is all there is to it.' So I let it be.

I felt so sorry for Charlie. He hadn't asked to be born like this. As if his life wasn't hard enough already without people making fun of him. After a long moment of silence, I tried to lift his spirits and suggested a game of Pictionary for two. Charlie seemed to cheer up from it. The evening turned out to be very nice with lots of jokes and laughter. Charlie left at about 10pm as it was a school day next day.

Lying in the dark in bed at night, I still shared his pain.

Tuesday, September 28th, 2004
Biosafety Level 2 Laboratory, unknown location

The men from the 69th Army Regiment lined up to receive the intravenous injection with the live virus. Becker was the first to take the needle. He had insisted on being first, just in case something went wrong.

"Don't faint now, Gov," Kaminski said.

"Tell us if it hurts, Gov," Grover whined in a female-like voice.

"Gents, can we please act like adults," Dr. Bonnetti said. This was a momentous occasion for her, potentially the lead to a huge step up the ladder, and she didn't want to have it spoilt by silly remarks.

"Of course, Doc. Sorry," Becker said and frowned at his mates. They complied, but Grover had a hard time to suppress a giggle. Deep down, he was as nervous as hell. First of all, he didn't like needles. Secondly, he didn't like this whole 'messing with nature' thing. He respected nature with all his being and this messing about with DNA and the likes... it felt like raping nature. He had only signed up because everybody else had. Of course he wanted to help Becker's kid, that wasn't the issue, but to have something genetically modified injected into him that was supposed to change his body was not what he had had in mind, to be honest. Yet, there was no going back now. At least he wouldn't be alone, he would be with his comrades. He would give his life for them. Yet he sincerely hoped this was not necessary on this mission.

Dr. Bonnetti stuck a small fluff of cotton on the injection site with some surgical tape and told Becker to bend his arm to keep the pressure on it.

"Okay, next one," Dr. Bonnetti said.

Becker got out of the chair and Kaminski took his place. As soon as Becker stood behind the doctor, he pretended soundlessly to choke. All his mates laughed out loud, except for Grover.

"Please sit down in the observation area, Mr. Becker," Dr. Bonnetti said without looking up.

Becker straightened up. "Yes, Ma'am," he said and turned around to go to the observation lounge next door.

It was only a few meters to the door but by the time he reached it, his knees gave way underneath him and he stumbled. He could only keep upright by holding on to the door post. He threw a quick glance over his shoulder and saw his mates' attention shifting from Kaminski getting his injection to him.

"It's the beginning of the end," Becker said with a shrug and a laugh, pretending he had stumbled on purpose. The others laughed but not as enthusiastically as they had done only a few seconds ago.

When Becker sat in a comfy chair in the observation

lounge, he tried to make sense of what was happening to him. He had this woozy feeling in his head. A man with a big beard came over to him. The man pushed a button on the side of the chair and Becker's legs were lifted up. The man then hooked Becker's chest and head up with wires. Soon it became hard for Becker to stay awake. He felt extremely tired and could hardly keep his eyes open. All he wanted to do was sleep. He wondered if he'd been injected with a sedative and they were going to cut him open when he was out. He saw all the men of his team come into the room, one after the other. They were all quiet and went to sit in the comfy chairs without a word. Becker had struggled to stay awake for as long as possible, but by the time he knew all his friends were okay and still alive, the virus got the better of him and he drifted off to sleep.

Dr. Bonnetti checked the vitals of all the soldiers. "Steady as she goes," she said.

All the soldiers were by now hooked up to wires to retrieve as much medical data as possible. What the monitors showed was that they were in a deep sleep.

"Is that normal?" Walpole asked Dr. Bonnetti as he scratched his beard.

Walpole was a lab assistant. He had assisted many tests in the facility, but never one like this one. Never had the test subjects all gone so fast into a deep sleep after being injected with a virus. Years ago, when they were testing with LSD, some of the test subjects had gone absolutely mental. 'Those were the fun days,' he thought. These days the tests were all 'humane' and, in his opinion, very boring. Especially this one.

"Yes, all the lab animals showed the same reaction. The muscles need to grow, and they do this best when the individual is asleep. As soon as they wake up we will start the questionnaire and measure their muscle mass. Let me know as soon as the first one awakes." With that statement, Dr. Bonnetti left the room.

Walpole watched the sleeping soldiers for hours. It was such boring work. As he watched the men, he couldn't help but be jealous of them. Sporting a serious beer belly wasn't what he really wanted. It was just the thought of not being able to drink beer that kept him from even attempting to go to a gym and lose weight. If only he could be part of this test and gain muscles by sleeping.

One of the soldiers stirred. Walpole walked over to him and checked his heart rate on the monitor. The man was definitely waking up.

Becker opened his eyes and saw the man with the bushy beard standing next to him. The man just put his cell phone in his pocket and now put pen to paper on a clipboard.

"What is your name?" Walpole asked him.

"Becker," Becker said as he noted the wires attached to him. His gaze followed the wires to the heart rate monitor, which bleeped with a steady rhythm.

"Do you know what year it is?" Walpole asked while writing down Becker's answer.

"Two-thousand-and-four," Becker said, now looking around and seeing Kaminski stir as well.

"Can you tell me who the current President is," Walpole continued.

"What stupid questions are these," Becker said.

"Look mate, I didn't write them. I'm just doing my job here, so I would be grateful if you could answer them and I'll be out of your hair." Walpole looked sideways now and noted Grover also waking up. He took his cell out of his pocket again and repeated his text to Dr. Bonnetti. 'Where is that woman when you need her,' he thought.

After a few minutes, Dr. Bonnetti finally made an appearance.

"How are you feeling?" she asked Becker. She checked his eyes with a light and his pupils were contracting as per normal. His heart rate and breathing were fast though. There had to be a reason for this.

"I'm fine," Becker said. He didn't mention the intense pain he felt in his jaws. He didn't know why it was there and he didn't want to seem silly. He must have been grinding his teeth while he was out or something. What other explanation could there be?

Wednesday, September 29th, 2004
Bullsbrook

Two months of teaching had been tough, as I had known it was going to be. In my private interview with Mr. Finkle that first day, he had told me 'If you survive the first year, you can do anything.' It had sounded so easy. During my studies, I had made lesson plans and gathered science experiments I could do with the students. Unfortunately, the school didn't have much material to work with. It appeared that the previous science teacher hadn't been in favor of practical experience and had taught mostly out of textbooks. I basically had to start from scratch. I was glad to find some websites that gave 'kitchen experiments' that anybody could do at home to show scientific principles. So I had my students scavenge their kitchens at home for material. I loved doing experiments and, as expected, so did my students.

Not all experiments went as planned. I made a typical beginners mistake when I walked out of the classroom to retrieve some material I had forgotten to get from the store room before the lesson started. When I returned, one of the students had set a desk on fire with a Bunsen burner. There was a big commotion of course and Mr. Finkle gave me a serious reprimand when I told him what happened. The student was suspended for two days. I wasn't sure this would have the desired effect on the student, but I certainly learned my lesson.

Sue had fewer problems with her pupils. She was such a bubbly person. Everybody instinctively liked her, and nobody gave her any insubordination problems. Of course, there was much less chance of students starting a fire in her classroom than in mine. I had the notion that most of the male students had a crush on her, from year seven to year twelve. Sue didn't believe me when I told her my suspicions at first, until one of the students had put his hand on her butt while she was walking through the classroom during group work. She hadn't known how to react and had ignored the incident at the time. She came to my place that evening, terribly upset, and I advised her to tell Mr. Finkle about it. She didn't do it as she couldn't prove it had happened. It had been so busy and chaotic in the classroom at the time that she didn't think anybody else had noticed. Later she told me she had become a bit more distant from her students from that moment on, standing behind her desk most of the time while teaching. I couldn't blame her. I probably would do so too, if I didn't need to interact with my students so much more.

Not that anybody would like to touch my skinny butt.

Charlie had a completely different issue teaching. As

he had been working on his own for years, he struggled to have people around him asking for his attention all the time. One Friday night, he told us he found it stressful he had to make sure nobody injured himself during class and it made him tense and very short-tempered. Whether it was his behavior or not, the students respected him. It could also have been because he had a world of experience and he helped the kids make beautiful things, from drawings to sculptures to metal and wood work. I was amazed that none of the students gave him a hard time about him being of short stature. They accepted him as he was, without prejudice, unlike some of the teachers.

The overall experience the three of us had was that teaching was great. Despite the initial setbacks, it was great to interact with the children. It gave me a tremendous boost to see the light in the children's eyes sparkle as they learned something new. Even though I liked the experiments I did with the kids, I enjoyed class discussions the most. To have the students interact with each other, dispute each other's thoughts, give arguments, and interact. This was the world I loved; a world where people listened to each other and discussed other people's visions without instantly dismissing them because they were different.

If only the real world out there could be like this.

Wednesday, September 29th, 2004
Biosafety Level 2 Laboratory, unknown location

Late that evening, Becker got out of bed in the shared bedroom and went to the bathroom. He locked the door and stood himself in front of the sink. He inspected his mirror image and didn't think he looked any different. He leaned his hands on the edge of the sink and moved his face closer to the mirror. When he lifted his upper lip and saw the reflection of his teeth, he gasped. He stumbled backward and bumped into the post of the shower cubicle. In a reflex to stay upright, he grabbed the handle of the cubicle door and ripped it completely off. Having nothing to hold on to now, he fell on his butt on the floor, the broken handle in his hand. "What the fuck?" Becker said out loud.

"Everything okay in there?" he heard Kaminski say.

"Yeah, I'm fine. Just slipped on the wet floor." He got up and moved to the mirror again. He threw the door handle into the sink and with both hands lifted his upper lip. Now he was sure it wasn't a figment of his imagination. He really had canines a wolf would be proud of. No wonder his jaw had been so sore. "Bloody hell," he muttered.

A knock on the bathroom door made him jump. Becker let go of his lip and quickly picked up the door

45

handle, holding it behind his back. "I told you I'm fine!" he yelled.

"Sorry, Gov," Kaminski whispered from behind the closed door. "Can I talk to you for a sec?"

Becker frowned but opened the door. "What is it?"

Kaminski glanced back over his shoulder. When he was sure none of the other soldiers were awake, he pushed his way into the bathroom and closed the door behind him.

"What's up, Kaminski? You better have a bloody good reason to barge in here," Becker said as he took a step backward. He was still holding the door handle behind his back and thought it might come in handy if Kaminski was up to something stupid.

"Gov, I have a problem," Kaminski whispered. He didn't look Becker in the eye.

"Don't tell me you have a problem down under. You need to see somebody else for that."

"No, Gov, you have it all wrong! I haven't got a problem down there, I have a problem up here," and he pointed at his mouth. Kaminski opened his mouth wide and sported a perfect pair of fangs. "My jaw has been bloody painful all day and I can feel my teeth have grown. I feel like a vampire and I'm not sure what to do!" He had a desperate look in his eye.

Becker's mind was racing. So, he wasn't the only one whose teeth were growing. Could this be a side-effect from the virus? Was this supposed to happen? What were the implications? Could they use them in combat? Apart from the tiredness and the pain, he felt as strong as an ox.

"Gov, what do I do?" Kaminski wiped his hand over his ultra-short hair.

Becker had to put his man at ease and there was only one way.

"Don't worry," he said. "Keep on smiling."

The man in front of him nodded a short nod and then realized what he had heard.

"Um… What? What did you say?" Kaminski asked.

"Just smile!" Becker said and made his grin as wide as possible, showing off his own pair of fangs.

"Oh my God! You have them too!" Kaminski said. Together they laughed.

There was knocking on the door again, this time louder.

"What is going on in there?" It was Grover's voice.

Becker opened the bathroom door and the two men stepped out.

Grover stood with his hands on his hips eying them suspiciously. "Having a secret meeting in there?" he asked.

"Grover, why don't you smile for a change?" Becker asked in return. He moved to put his hand on the man's shoulder but forgot he was still holding the door handle. He stopped his move midway, staring at the item, and realized it must look a bit awkward.

"What in heaven's name have you two been up to in there?" Grover asked, frowning at the broken piece of metal.

Becker laughed. "Well, it seems that the virus is working. I fell and trying to hold on to something, I took the handle off as easy as if it was made of butter."

"You're kidding?" Kaminski said.

"Nope, I swear on my mother's grave. It came right off when I grabbed it," Becker said.

The three of them laughed and Becker didn't fail to notice Grover also had a nice set of wolf-like canines.

Becker woke the three remaining sleeping men in the room as well as the five next door. They all appeared to have long canines. The men gathered around Becker.

"What does it mean, Gov?" Johnsson asked. He was the youngest of the troop. "Are we turning into animals?"

"Would the Doc know this would happen, you think," Kaminski asked.

"I really don't think so,' Becker replied. "Turning into animals is a bit far-fetched and I don't think the Doc knows. Otherwise, she would have monitored the growth of our fangs."

Suddenly the light turned on and all the men had to blink. When they focused to see who had flipped the switch, they saw Walpole standing in the doorway.

Wednesday, September 29th, 2004
Biosafety Level 2 Laboratory, unknown location

Walpole's big frame was impressive, filling most of the doorway.

"What's going on, guys?" Walpole said as he scuffed his beard. "The night guard told me he saw you wandering in the hallway on the cameras. Is anything wrong?"

Becker was confused. Looking at Walpole made him thirsty, very thirsty. He couldn't see the man's jugular through his beard, but it was as if he could hear it. It was almost as if he could hear the blood sloshing through the man's veins. Warm, liquid, thirst-quenching blood. The thought scared the hell out of him. Yet, he took a step closer toward the man.

"No, nothing's wrong," he said. From the corner of his eye, he saw Kaminski flank him on the right, Grover was not far behind on the left. Both men took another step closer to Walpole. "Nothing's wrong at all."

"Then why are you all out of bed?" Walpole asked as he shuffled back into the hallway. He didn't like the look on the men's faces. The eyes were too intent. He glanced quickly at the cameras hanging in the corners of the hallway. Looking back at Becker, he said, "Do you want me to call Dr. Bonnetti?"

49

Walpole put his hand into the pocket of his lab coat, but when he found nothing, he realized he had left his cell phone lying on the nightstand. 'Damn, this isn't good,' he thought.

Becker had noticed the big man looking away at the cameras and quickly assessed the situation. He jumped forward and grabbed Walpole by the lapels of his coat. He pulled the heavy frame of the bearded man into the room and closed the door behind him. When Becker's eyes met Kaminski's, he realized his mate's eyes were asking. They weren't asking what was going on. They were asking for permission. Becker blinked. Kaminski was asking him permission to kill Walpole. He had seen the look in the soldiers' eyes before, just before a kill when they were on duty in Iraq. Only this time, Kaminski's stare was so much more intense. Absolutely no doubt about it. The man wanted to kill, just like he did himself.

Walpole threw a glance at the door. He thought of saying something but refrained from it as he didn't believe these guys had any intention of listening to anybody at the moment.

'This isn't going to end well,' Walpole thought to himself.

The blow came out of nowhere and Walpole was unconscious before he hit the floor. He never woke up again because the men of the 69th battalion immediately fell on him and quenched their thirst.

Becker wiped the blood off his chin. He got up and Kaminski and Johnsson joined him. Most of the others were still trying to get the last drop out of Walpole.

"What have we done?" moaned Grover, who stood looking at the white corpse, his fists clenched to his cheeks. "What on earth have we done?"

Becker thought exactly the same thing. He hadn't wanted to kill Walpole, but his thirst had taken over. His body had demanded to take action to quench this immense need and killing Walpole and relieving him of his blood had been the obvious solution. He wasn't proud of it, but what was done was done. He realized his career was shot. He could hand himself in, but that would mean a dishonest discharge and they would probably do everything in their power to cancel the side-effect of the virus in him. That was something he couldn't let happen. Not while he felt so fucking good. He felt like his body was changing for the better, into some sort of super human. Why would he want to go back to what he had been before?

"We're doomed! We're all doomed!" wailed Grover in the meantime. The soldier was now pacing the room, shaking everyone by the shoulders.

Becker turned his head to Grover and sighed. Johnsson took this as a sign to take action. He grabbed Grover and pushed him up against the wall, his lower arm pressing against the man's throat.

"You want me to take care of him?" Kaminski asked

Becker.

After a short moment, Becker gave the slightest nod upon which Kaminski moved to Grover and Johnsson.

"Grover, are you going to shut up?" he asked.

Grover stopped whimpering. He stared at Kaminski intently before he talked.

"You're evil! We're all evil! We're all going to hell!" he yelled into Kaminski's face, who kept surprisingly calm.

"No worries, mate, I've already been there and back again,' he said as he indicated to Johnsson to let go of Grover. "Why don't we go and find the Doc, okay? She can sort out this mess."

Kaminski put his arm around Grover's shoulders and led his fellow soldier toward the door. They were about three paces away from it when Kaminski put both hands on the sides of Grover's head and broke his neck.

Johnsson stared at the body of his mate in horror as Becker addressed the rest of the men.

"Anybody else wants out? No? Good. Now listen up. We have to get out of here, and fast. If we stay, we're doomed like Grover said. We're going to extract ourselves out of this hostile situation. And don't get me wrong, this will be a hostile situation as soon as they find out we killed these men. Kaminski, get Walpole's key card. We're going to visit our security friend first.

Wednesday, September 29th, 2004
Biosafety Level 2 Laboratory, unknown location

Ricardo Ricci sat with his feet on his desk. He was filling in a crossword puzzle when his eye caught movement again on one of the monitors. He lazily glanced up at it, expecting Walpole returning. Instead, he saw the group of soldiers walking his way.

"Now what?" he said as he moved his feet off the desk.

A few minutes earlier, he had woken the fat bastard Walpole because he had seen his test bunnies roaming the hallway in the middle of the night. He thought they probably had the shits or something. During the few years as a guard here, nothing exciting ever seemed to happen, which was just the way he liked it. What had gone wrong that Walpole wasn't with the soldiers? Ricci got out of his chair and opened the door of his office.

"Hey, guys, what's up?" he asked as the soldiers approached. Just in case, he had taken the clip off his hip holster and kept his hand on the gun.

Before Ricci had a chance to move Becker rushed up to him and bit Ricci's neck, sucking at his jugular. Ricci screamed his lungs out. He didn't have a chance getting his gun out as Becker wasn't a fool and had twisted

Ricci's arm behind his back when he attacked. The man was as strong as an ox and Ricci couldn't move one way or another. After a minute or so, Becker let go of Ricci, taking the gun out of its holster as he did. Shaking on his legs and clutching at his neck, Ricci stared at the men who were staring at Becker.

"Why didn't you kill him?" Kaminski asked.

"Why would I?" Becker replied. He was a trained killer, but he didn't see the need to kill innocent people if he could help it. He had bitten the man as that had been the fastest way to disarm him. Besides, he may be of more use to them alive.

"How do we get out of here?" Becker asked Ricci.

Ricci didn't say anything. However, Becker did see the man's eyes go to the door at the far end of the hallway.

"Look, this is the situation," Becker told Ricci. "We're going to get out of here, whether you like it or not. You can come with us or we will kill you. Your choice." Becker stared into the guard's eyes.

Ricci was no fool. He had a sense of duty, sure, but he knew a lost cause when he saw one. Sticking to his patriotism at this very moment was one of those.

"You can't get out, you need two key cards," he said, "and I only have one.

At this, Kaminski smiled a broad grin and showed Ricci the card he had taken from Walpole.

Ricci led the men to the car park. There weren't

many cars there, but enough to get the men out. Becker made the sign to gather and waited until every soldier was within hearing distance.

"Okay, listen up. This is it. This is where we split our ways. As soon as you leave this car park, you're on your own. You're trained to survive and that's what you're going to do. This is a life or death situation. *Your* life or death. Go out, sleep during the day, travel by night. It's the best chance you have of staying under the radar. Speed and power!"

"Speed and power!" came the unanimous reply.

As the men spread out into the world, so did the virus.

Friday, October 8th, 2004
Bullsbrook

On Friday evenings you could always find us in the Celtic Frog, the local bar in Bullsbrook. It was owned by Enrique, a French guy with a Spanish name. He reminded me a bit of that guy from the funny TV series 'Alo, alo', what was his name again? Ah, René, that was it. Enrique was also a bit chubby, with a receding hairline, and he thought the ladies quite liked him. However, in contrast to René in the series who couldn't keep the women at bay, Enrique didn't attract the attention he so imagined. Miraculously though, he was married to a really gorgeous, Celtic woman, named Abby. Her real name was Abigail, but everybody called her Abby. She was a voluptuous, big lipped, red-haired lady. She was very chatty and definitely in charge of the place; 'au contraire' of what Enrique thought. Because of their names, we often planned our get-togethers for the Friday night at the 'A&E', coincidentally also the English term for the 'Accidents & Emergencies' department in hospitals, instead of using the pub's name. We received some funny looks from bystanders when we did that and we never told anybody what we meant, which made it extra special.

Charlie was ordering another round of beer for us

when we heard about suckers for the first time. Sue and I were watching the news on the TV in the corner when Charlie returned from the bar with his hands full.

"Listen to this, Charlie," Sue said.

"Yeah, please take this out of my hands first, my lady, and I will do your bidding" he replied. Charlie always pretended to be Sue's jester. Sue didn't think anything of it, but I always thought that Charlie wanted to be more than that to her.

We quickly took our beers from him, raised them, and said 'All for one and one for all.' We took a big gulp of the cool, golden liquid and the three of us turned our heads to the TV screen. The newsreader just ended her sentence with '...disturbing images' and then we were shown footage of what was happening in Portland. We saw people being chased by others and, quite dramatically, being bitten in the neck. The images were a bit vague as it was all filmed in the dark.

"New vampire movie coming out?" Charlie asked.

"No! This is for real! This is really happening, man," I blurted out.

"You're kidding me," he replied with disbelief written all over his face.

"It's true," I said, "Otherwise they wouldn't show it on the news now, would they?" And I took another big gulp of my beer.

The drunk-one has spoken.

Charlie stared at me, then at Sue.

"You're kidding me," he repeated.

I could understand his reaction. The images on TV seemed so unreal. Like a war in some far away country that didn't affect our personal lives in the slightest, and this war being paranormal fiction too instead of real. Sue and I stared back at Charlie with big eyes.

"Wow! That's unreal. Is it bad?" he finally said.

"Only if you get killed apparently," I informed him, "If you live you get to be a vampire."

"Cool!" he grinned, "But I am sure you mean 'if you die, you get to be a vampire." He finally sat down.

I thought about what the newsreader had said on the news. I was pretty sure she'd said you became a sucker when you survived an attack.

"That's confusing," I frowned.

Both Sue and Charlie laughed.

After we had a bit of contemplation and some more beer, Sue asked, "Would you get to live forever you think?"

"Well, that would be awkward, with the shortage of housing in the city already," I quipped.

Sue and Charlie burst out laughing.

"What?" I asked them. "It's true, isn't it? There *is* a housing shortage."

"You always look at things from a practical point of view, don't you?" Charlie said as he stomped me playfully on my arm.

And the conversation drifted to the housing

58

problems our college friends were having in the big cities. That conversation seemed so much more important than blood-sucking people at the time.

Monday, October 11th, 2004
Bullsbrook

The three of us didn't watch any more news that weekend as we were all too busy making teaching plans and strategies for the coming week. When we arrived in the staffroom on Monday morning, there was a buzz with news about vampires, chaos, and death. Mrs. Sloan, the history teacher, was crying and snottering while others tried to calm her down. Apparently, her daughter was lost; she lived in Portland. Other teachers stood in little groups, whispering, as if in a conspiracy about something. Charlie wasn't there as he always went straight to his classroom in the morning. His excuse was that he needed time to set up equipment for the first lesson, but I knew better.

When Mr. Finkle emerged from his office and entered the staff room, everybody became quiet and looked at him for guidance. He wasn't a bulky man nor particularly handsome, more of a weasel really, and as such didn't entice any respect from his looks. However, as he stood there, with his hands on his hips waiting for everybody to be quiet, he knew that we would listen to him. He was after all the Head Teacher. It was obvious from the grin on his face that he enjoyed this role. He changed his facial features to a more serious one.

"I know they say there is a grave situation going on. However, I don't want to give in to mass hysteria. We must think of the children. We mustn't worry them with grown-up's problems." His gaze went around the room again. "Therefore, we'll continue teaching and not talk about it at all in the school."

The majority of teachers nodded in agreement and told each other 'not to worry the children.' Mrs. Sloan burst out into another crying session, her morbidly obese frame shaking with every sob.

Mr. Finkle's speech blew my mind.

This is such old-fashioned ostrich policy!

I raised my arm in protest, but Sue grabbed it before my hand went past my head and held it down. I turned to her, frowning.

"It's of no use," she whispered, "nobody will listen."

I looked around and saw everybody already leaving the staff room as if nothing had happened.

"We'll talk at lunchtime," Sue said as she left for her class as well.

Over the next few days, it became clear that this epidemic was actually a pandemic. On TV they showed us reports of attacks coming from all over the world and they said that the number of victims was rising steeply. I thought this terminology of 'victims' was very inappropriate. These suckers don't seem in the least disabled, physically or mentally.

It appeared that somehow the affliction had spread

under the radar and had burst out all over the planet. They couldn't find patient zero. At first, they didn't know whether it was caused by bacteria or a virus or something new entirely. Some quickly-done research made it clear it was caused by a virus. A bioscientist on TV told the public they named the unknown virus the '*Succedaneum*' virus as this meant 'substitute.' The virus didn't turn people into the living dead but into another, blood-sucking form of humans. People began calling them 'suckers' from then on.

Is this disease finally going to be the end of humanity?

When not teaching, we were glued to the TV screen, hungry for more information. Little by little more information was released.

Next, they told us that the suckers had their own form of 'kryptonite'; it was sunlight. They were extremely photo-sensitive. We already knew that they were shunning daylight and only coming out at night, but they hadn't told us why in the beginning. It appeared that when exposed to sunlight, they would instantly have an epileptic seizure, the full tonic-clonic one. You never saw movies where vampires had epileptic seizures when they were exposed to sunlight. They usually disintegrated into a pile of dust, some faster than others, depending on which movie you were watching and what budget they had been able to acquire. I pointed out they would have to clean up whole bodies now, instead of using a brush and dustpan, which was going to be a lot more costly. Charlie and Sue nearly rolled on the floor laughing. It was a release of tension we all needed badly. It wasn't so funny when they showed us images on the TV of suckers having epileptic seizures when exposed to the sun.

On Thursday it all of a sudden became very close to home for me and so much more real; I couldn't contact my parents anymore. They didn't pick up the phone, weren't online, and they didn't own any cell phones. Earlier in the week I had told them to come to my place, but they insisted it was just a fad and that it would soon fly over. I became afraid of their fate. I wanted to jump in my car and drive home. Sue and Charlie fortunately physically stopped me and argued that it would be senseless as the army had closed off the roads into and out of the cities, trying to contain the situation. So I frantically tried to contact my sisters, to find out if they were okay and if they had heard anything from Mom and Dad. This had no result either. The naval base Maxine was living on was probably in lockdown and I felt relief in the thought that at least she would be safe. I couldn't get a hold of Julie, which worried me. Her cell phone kept going to answering machine mode. As she was living in a country town not far from me she was probably okay. She probably just forgot to charge her cell.

She is a very self-sufficient girl, I shouldn't worry about her.

Sue couldn't get a hold of her family either and to drive south would be too dangerous. Charlie didn't have any real family to be worried about. His parents had died years ago in a car accident and he wasn't in contact with his aunt, his only living relative. He didn't even know where she lived.

By Friday all communications had stopped. During the week, one TV station after another had ceased to broadcast. Then the radio went silent. The internet still worked, so to speak, but there were no broadcasts, no news flashes. Less and less people tried to contact one another. People giving out locations of safe places ceased to communicate, and we could only speculate that the suckers had followed their directions. By this time, Bullsbrook was in total chaos. People were rampaging through town. Some were trying to fortify their houses, some were plundering the supermarkets for food, and others were looting as much as they could. As if a large flat screen TV could save you from suckers.

THE END

LIVING LIKE A VAMPIRE
Book 1

Kate is trying very hard to stay alive in a world thrown into chaos. Charlie is trying very hard to get Kate to notice him. When Caleb comes to the scene, things change, but is it for the better?

Kate had just begun her new job as a high school science teacher and was looking forward to living a suburban dream life. All her hopes and dreams turn into smoke as a virus turns people into vampires roaming the world in packs and killing everybody they can get their hands on. Together with her friends Sue and Charlie, she hides at a campground. They think they are safe there. They are wrong.

They are attacked by a pack of suckers and Kate has to flee again. She gets separated from her friends, accidentally bumps into a handsome sucker who then mysteriously disappears, after which she has to pretend to be a sucker to stay alive. Having met Caleb, surviving is no longer the only thing on Kate's mind.

RAISING A VAMPIRE
Book 2

Kate and her little family have led a quiet life. An unfortunate event sees Kate following her daughter into prison. Events drive the happy family apart.

One day, Kate makes the mistake to invite a colleague into her home. He betrays her trust and commits an act of violence. When Kate's daughter comes to the rescue, she exposes herself for what she really is; a sucker. Kate accompanies her daughter when she is sent to a sucker internment camp. The situation quickly spirals downhill when an old flame from the past turns up and rekindles Kate's love for him.

Once more, Kate is thrown into turmoil and heartache.

Join Kate as she struggles with the amorous feelings that awaken after meeting her old flame. Feel her pain as she loses the friendship of a good friend, as she pushes her daughter away from her instead of keeping her on the right path, and as she tries to stay faithful to her partner.

Can Kate keep her family and her wits together?

KILLING A VAMPIRE
Book 3

The past is back to haunt Kate. Will her partner survive this evil?

Kate thinks her relationship is on the rocks because of her past infidelity. She's wrought with guilt and wants nothing more than her missing partner back. When the police don't believe there's foul play at hand she's on her own to find him. A horrifying parcel arriving on Kate's doorstep brings the situation to a whole new lever. The police are now willing but can't due to lack of evidence.

There is one person able to help Kate, but everybody warns her not to accept his helping hand. How far is Kate willing to go to save the one she loves?

Killing a Vampire explores the emotional bonds between mother and child, sisters, and lovers. Follow the hints and clues as Kate explores the depth of her emotions while trying to save her love.

About the Author

Jacky Dahlhaus has worked many jobs and tried many hobbies before she realized writing gave her such pleasure. She loves to write paranormal fantasy stories while delving into the human psyche with all its faults and mysteries.

Next to writing novels, Jacky helps indie authors by promoting them on her blog, writes an online newsletter/magazine, runs a writing club for adults and for children at the local library, and is a director for Aberdeenshire Film Productions.

When not busy with the above (which is rare nowadays), Jacky works on renovating her Scottish Victorian home, watches movies with her family, and tries to stop her two Jack Russells from barking for no good reason.

Releasing A Vampire is her first novelette and the prequel to the Suckers trilogy.

jackydahlhaus.com

Connect

I'd love to hear from you!
You can connect with me via:

Email:
jackydahlhaus@gmail.com

Twitter:
https://twitter.com/JackyDahlhaus

Instagram:
https://www.instagram.com/jackydahlhaus/

Facebook:
https://www.facebook.com/Jacky-Dahlhaus-Author-166614624053352/

My Website:
https://jackydahlhaus.com

Thank you so much for reading, and I hope to read your review soon, see your name on my mailing list, and be able to send you my next book!

Jacky Dahlhaus

Acknowledgements

Half of this story was part of the original *Living Like A Vampire* novel. Hence I would like to thank the people that helped me write that story. This includes my close friends Suzie, Bob, Chris, and Stephanie. It also includes Dr. Chloe Alexander of Aberdeen University as well as my Mom and my author friends from the Once Stop Fiction Authors' Resource Facebook Group; Colin, Terry, and Joy. I thank you all from the bottom of my heart.

I thank my children and my husband, who had to forgo my company during the evenings I was writing. I love you so much!

Jacky Dahlhaus